Maud and Grand-Maud

For my editor, Maria Modugno, whose grandmother Marie
called her Mariucci (little Marie). And in memory of my
much-loved grandmothers, Ruby and Sadie, who've been
gone a long time and who are always with me. —S.O.

For my aunt 원정순 —K.P.

Text copyright © 2020 by Sara O'Leary
Jacket art and interior illustrations copyright © 2020 by Kenard Pak

All rights reserved. Published in the United States by Random House
Children's Books, a division of Penguin Random House LLC, New York.
Published simultaneously in Canada by Tundra Books, an imprint of
Penguin Random House Canada Young Readers,
a Penguin Random House Company, in 2020.

Random House and the colophon are registered trademarks of
Penguin Random House LLC.

Visit us on the Web! rhcbooks.com

Educators and librarians, for a variety of teaching tools, visit us at
RHTeachersLibrarians.com

Library of Congress Cataloging-in-Publication Data
Names: O'Leary, Sara, author. | Pak, Kenard, illustrator.
Title: Maud and Grand-Maud / by Sara O'Leary ; illustrated by Kenard Pak.
Description: New York : Random House Children's Books, [2020] | Audience:
Ages 3–7. | Audience: Grades K–1. | Summary: Maud's weekends with her
grandmother include matching nightgowns, breakfast for supper, old movies,
special surprises, and dreams of becoming Grand-Maud herself, one day.
Identifiers: LCCN 2019027627 (print) | LCCN 2019027628 (ebook) |
ISBN 978-0-399-55458-2 (hardcover) | ISBN 978-0-399-55459-9 (library binding) |
ISBN 978-0-399-55460-5 (ebook)
Subjects: CYAC: Grandmothers—Fiction. | Sleepovers—Fiction.
Classification: LCC PZ7.O46257 Mau 2020 (print) | LCC PZ7.O46257 (ebook) | DDC [E]—dc23

MANUFACTURED IN CHINA
10 9 8 7 6 5 4 3 2 1
First U.S. Edition

MAUD AND GRAND-MAUD

By SARA O'LEARY   Illustrated by KENARD PAK

Random House 🏠 New York

On special Saturdays, Maud goes to Grand-Maud's house and doesn't go home until Sunday.

Maud worries a little about leaving her parents on their own, but Grand-Maud says she thinks they will be all right.

Grand-Maud has made Maud a nightgown for the nights she sleeps over. The nightgown goes all the way to the floor, and is made out of plaid flannel, and is softer than anything.

But what makes the nightgown special is that Grand-Maud
has made herself one to match.

Once Maud and Grand-Maud have put on their nightgowns, they are ready to have breakfast for supper. "No matter what you like to eat for breakfast, it somehow always tastes better at suppertime," says Maud.

Because it is just the two of them, they eat their breakfast for supper on trays in the living room and watch movies.

They will watch any kind of movie as long as it is in black and white.

"Was everything black and white when you were small?"
Maud asks.

"What do you think?" says Grand-Maud.

Maud pictures her grandmother as a little girl.
"Oh yes," she says.

When it is time for bed, Maud sleeps in the same room as Grand-Maud because there are twin beds and one of them is just for Maud.

The bed is a special bed. Not just because Maud always has good dreams when she sleeps in it, though she always does.

The bed is special because there is an old wooden chest underneath and there is always something new for Maud placed inside, even when Grand-Maud doesn't know she will be visiting.

Sometimes the chest holds something bought from a shop, like a toy or a treat or a set of watercolor paints.

Even better, the chest may hold something Grand-Maud
has made for Maud, like a sweater, or a pair of mittens, or some
cookies to take home so the time between visits is sweeter.

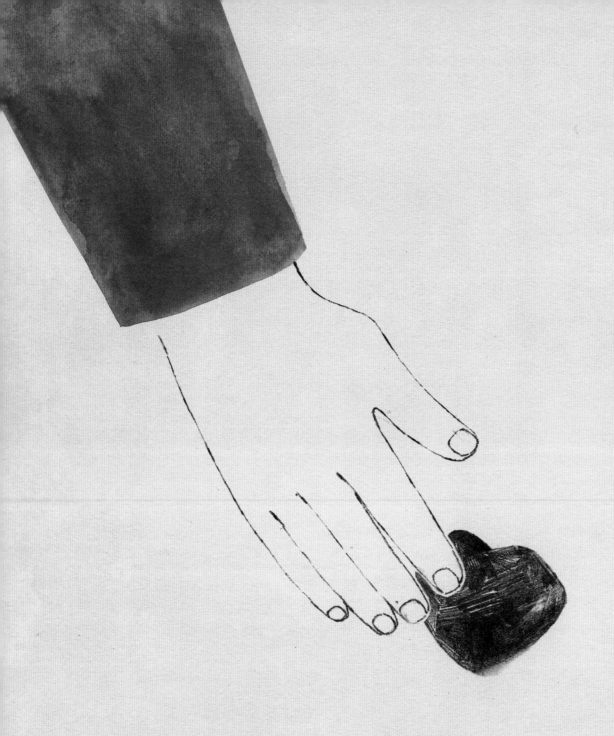

Best of all is when the chest has something from when
Grand-Maud was a little girl herself.

One time, the chest held a stone shaped like a heart.

"I carried that in my pocket for one whole year," said
Grand-Maud. "It went everywhere I went."

Maud is happy to carry it in her own pocket wherever she goes now.

Another time, there was a picture of Grand-Maud
riding on an elephant.

"You never told me you rode on a real elephant,"
said Maud.

"You never asked," said Grand-Maud.

This time, there is a book of fairy tales with Maud's name written in cursive inside it.
"This book has my name in it," says Maud.

"I wasn't Grand-Maud until you were born,"
says her grandmother. "Once upon a time, I was
just Maud."

Before Maud goes to sleep, Grand-Maud sits on the next
bed and dims the light. She then asks Maud questions
about what she thinks her life will be like.

"When I grow up," says Maud, "I am going to write the kind
of stories that go in books. But they will all be happy stories.
Some will be about people and some might be about cats."

"Will you have children?" asks Grand-Maud.

"Oh yes. Seven children."

"Seven!" says Grand-Maud.

"At least seven," says Maud. "And we will live in a very tall house so that the children can have bunk beds that go up and up and up."

"And then one day, you will have a granddaughter of your own," says Grand-Maud.

Maud smiles into the dark.

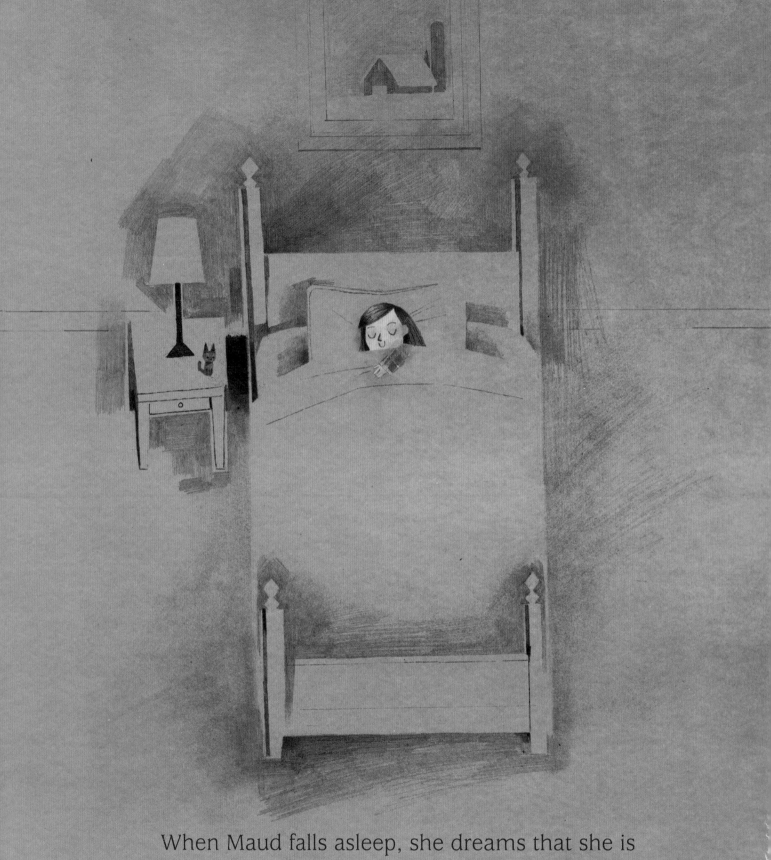

When Maud falls asleep, she dreams that she is
Grand-Maud and lives in an apartment building
and has a bedroom with twin beds.

And in the dream, she is just waiting for one of
Maud's special visits.